My Delicious Garden

Written by Anne-Marie Fortin
Illustrated by Julien Castanié

Translated by Heather Camlot

Owlkids Books

JANUARY
The year has just begun.
While I watch the snow fall,
I'm already imagining
the great big garden of my dreams.

I can't wait for the month of May,
when tangy rhubarb,
the groundbreaker,
will push through the surface of the soil.

FEBRUARY

How big will my garden be?
Bigger than last year!
Smaller than next year ...
One day, we'll run out of room!

I draw up a plan.
One row of lettuces won't be enough!
I picture a trellis for the climbing peas.
And the tomatoes will get the biggest plot of all.

MARCH

Finally, it's time for sowing!
I plant small seeds inside eggshells:
peppers, leeks, and celery
will sprout in just a few days.

My moms insist on labeling everything.
Last year, we forgot what we planted,
and the red tomatoes turned out to be purple!
Each new surprise made me laugh.

APRIL

The first leaves of my seedlings
search for spring's light.
The roots want to stretch,
but the shells are now too small.

Quickly, I repot them into bigger containers.
The seedlings will grow strong
in a soil rich with nutrients
and produce yummy vegetables!

MAY

The soil has finally warmed up,
and the perennials start to grow.
When the chives and mint spread out in the sunshine,
it's time to get my hands dirty!

As we ready the garden for planting,
I feel like a queen taking care of my land!
My moms spread the compost and turn up the soil.
I plant and water and listen to the birds sing.

JUNE

I inspect my garden every day.
While I weed and water, I watch for the first flowerings.
And I make scary faces to chase away
squirrels, groundhogs, and slugs.

Some days feel longer than others.
I just want to eat some melon!
Instead, to pass the time,
I crunch on the first crisp radishes.

JULY

We start the harvest—
my favorite season has begun!
We still have plenty of fruits and vegetables,
even though animals have been nibbling on them.

In the morning, I pick bright red raspberries.
At lunch, I dig up an onion.
By late afternoon, the kitchen smells like raspberry pie.
In the evening, Mom says: "Go pick a cabbage, quick!"

AUGUST

The hot sun and the rain
help my broccoli grow.
Eggplant, carrots, and zucchini
color each tasty dish.

By the end of the summer, we have a bounty!
Even if we feast every day,
there is still enough fennel, cucumbers, and rosemary
to share with our neighbors.

SEPTEMBER

The days get shorter
as summer gives way to fall.
Even though some plants have died off,
we still harvest leeks by the ton!

Calling all cooks to the kitchen!
With marinades, jams, and pickles
stored in the pantry,
we'll enjoy our harvest all year round.

OCTOBER

The leaves have fallen,
the geese are gone.
The garden is closed,
the harvest is done.

But the largest and most beautiful
and most orange of all my pumpkins
is ready when my friends
gather for a costume party!

NOVEMBER

The first snow has settled
on my delicious garden.
I remember my dirty hands and black fingernails—
and then I run outside to play in the snow!

When it's cold and gray,
and the garden is at rest,
I go down to the cellar and grin:
tonight, we'll eat a yummy stew!

DECEMBER

On a festive table,
my moms have arranged
all our summer treasures:
fruit ketchup,
marinated beets,
sweet pickles,
baby potatoes,
roasted carrots,
braised turnip.

And we are treated
to smiles from our guests.

To Clémence,
my favorite gardener, for all the vegetable gardens to come
— A.F.

To Laurence,
for the seasons that have passed and those that remain
— J.C.

Text © 2019 Anne-Marie Fortin
Illustrations © 2019 Julien Castanié
English translation © 2022 Owlkids Books
Originally published as *Mon Beau Potager* by Éditions de l'Isatis

Published in Canada by Owlkids Books Inc., 1 Eglinton Avenue East, Toronto, ON M4P 3A1
Published in the United States by Owlkids Books Inc., 1700 Fourth Street, Berkeley, CA 94710

Owlkids Books acknowledges the financial support of the Canada Council for the Arts, the Ontario Arts Council, the Government of Canada through the Canada Book Fund (CBF) and the Government of Ontario through the Ontario Creates Book Initiative for our publishing activities.

Library and Archives Canada Cataloguing in Publication

Title: My delicious garden / written by Anne-Marie Fortin ; illustrated by Julien Castanié.
Other titles: Mon beau potager. English
Names: Fortin, Anne-Marie, author. | Castanié, Julien, 1983- illustrator.
 | Camlot, Heather, translator.
Description: Translation of: Mon beau potager. Translated by: Heather Camlot.
Identifiers: Canadiana 20210212403 | ISBN 9781771474689 (hardcover)
Subjects: LCSH: Vegetable gardening—Juvenile fiction. | LCSH: Gardening—Juvenile fiction. | LCSH:
    Vegetables—Juvenile fiction. | LCSH: Seasons—Juvenile fiction. | LCGFT: Picture books.
Classification: LCC PS8611.O7747 M6613 2022 | DDC jC843/.6—dc23

Library of Congress Control Number: 2021939046

ONTARIO ARTS COUNCIL
CONSEIL DES ARTS DE L'ONTARIO
an Ontario government agency
un organisme du gouvernement de l'Ontario

Canada Council
for the Arts
Conseil des Arts
du Canada

Canadä

Manufactured in Guangdong Province, Dongguan City, China, in September 2021, by Toppan Leefung
Job #BAYDC99

A   B   C   D   E   F

FSC
MIX
Paper from
responsible sources
FSC® C104723
www.fsc.org

Publisher of Chirp, Chickadee and OWL
www.owlkidsbooks.com

Owlkids Books is a division of bayard canada